Loxley's Locs

www.nubianamedia.com

Loxley's Locs

Be unapologetically authentic.
Be proud of who you are.
Wear your natural hair with pride,
And sparkle like a star!

-Samantha Rodgers

Loxley had enchanting locs,
They flowed majestically.
Each strand brimmed with mighty strength,
And twisted impressively.

Adorned with a mixture of natural oils,
And hypnotic scents of cologne,
They inhabited every inch of his scalp,
Enjoying a life of their own.

Loxley loved his magnificent locs.
He was such a regal boy.
He cherished his crowning glory.
They are his pride and joy.

But his locs caused a matter of contention,
At his brand new school,
When the headteacher informed his parents,
That his hairstyle breached their rules.

They said his locs were unacceptable,
And he needed to cut his hair,
But his parents vehemently objected,
And protested that this was unfair.

Loxley was raised to be proud of his locs,
Without feeling the need to conform,
To eurocentric standards,
In order to fit the norm.

His school finally acknowledged,
That they had no right to dictate,
How Loxley should wear his natural hair.
They were wrong to discriminate.

Sadly, this was not the only time,
That Loxley would have to face,
Issues with his hairstyle.
They were unfortunately commonplace.

His locs attracted attention,
And caused people to stare,
As they looked on in admiration,
At the wonders of his hair.

Some were totally mesmerised,
But often showed a lack of care,
As they eagerly beckoned towards him,
In an attempt to touch his hair.

He knew that people were curious,
About how his locs would feel,
But they would often be intrusive,
Not thinking it was such a big deal.

One day, when Loxley was at school,
His friend tried to touch his hair.
He didn't ask for permission,
And this caused Loxley despair.

Loxley quickly pulled away,
He was clearly not amused,
But his friend didn't seem to understand,
And looked really confused.

Loxley's parents always told him,
That his hair was his personal space,
And that no one had the given right,
To invade this sacred place.

He did not like trespassing hands,
So demanded that others refrain,
From asking if they could touch his hair,
Again and again and again.

So Loxley was always ready,
To confidently block,
Any inquisitive hands,
Diving in to feel his locs.

Eventually, people left his hair alone,
They understood that it was not okay,
To intrude in his locs uninvited,
Even in an admiring way.

As Loxley's locs grew longer,
Swinging along to his every beat,
He walked with pride triumphantly,
His locs made him feel complete.

His locs are truly spectacular,
Everyone adores them so much,
But now they know the golden rule,
You can look but please don't touch.

Printed in Great Britain
by Amazon